THERE'S A BEAR IN THE BATHROOM

written by
Susan F. Smith

illustrated by
Maggie Weir

Eifrig Publishing LLC
Berlin   Lemont

Published by Eifrig Publishing,
PO Box 66, Lemont, PA 16851, USA
Knobelsdorffstr. 44, 14059 Berlin, Germany.

For information regarding permission, write to:
Rights and Permissions Department,
Eifrig Publishing, LLC
PO Box 66, Lemont, PA 16851, USA.
permissions@eifrigpublishing.com, +1-888-340-6543

Library of Congress Control Number: 2010929339

Smith, Susan Fernald, 1940-
      There's a Bear in the Bathroom /by Susan F. Smith
      illustrated by Maggie Weir
p. cm.

Paperback: ISBN 978-1-936172-10-8
Hardcover: ISBN 978-1-936172-18-4

    I. Weir, Maggie ill. II. Title: There's a Bear in the Bathroom
    III. Animal tale

2016 15 14 13 12
5 4 3 2 1

Printed on acid-free paper. ∞

Dedicated to four
sparkling grandkids,
Eliot, Saede,
Safi, and Casie —
S. F. S.

"There's a bear in the bathroom,"
I let out a shout.

"There's a bear in the bathroom,
And she won't come out!"

Where did she come from?
Who could she be?

How she got into OUR house
is what worried me!

7

As I peeked in the door
she was taking a shower.

From the looks of the room
she'd been in there an hour.

Who ever heard
of a bear in the shower?

Using all of mom's soap,
she smelled like a flower!

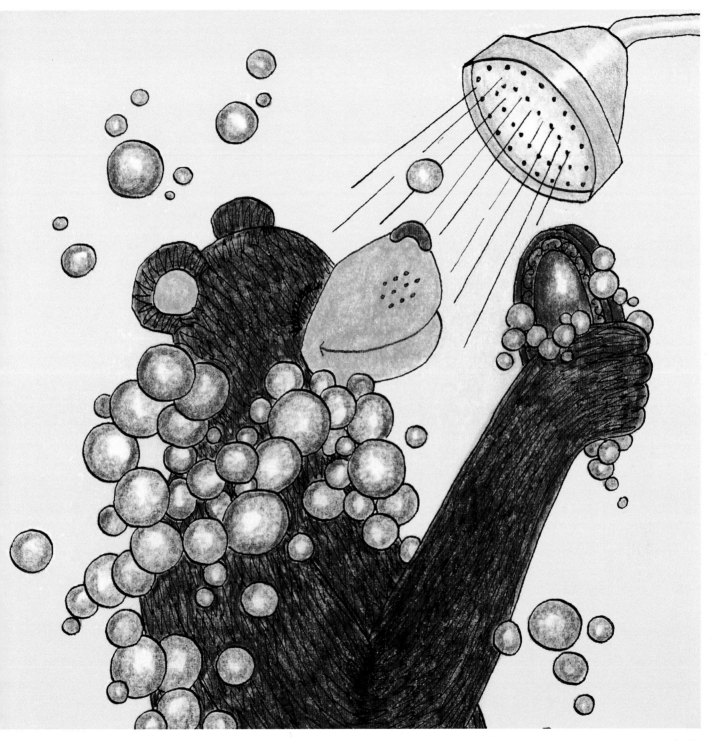

The next thing, I thought,
she'll be brushing her teeth.

And she did, glory be,
with a smile underneath!

My sis won't believe it,
or my mom or my dad.

They'll just think it's another
strange dream that I've had.

But wait till they see
the big tracks on the floor,

And the big dirty paw prints
outside of the door.

17

18

Her paws are all clean now,
after all of that rubbing.

Now it's the BATHROOM
that needs a good scrubbing!

I'll wait till she's gone
and then tell my folks.

They'll probably think
it's just one of my jokes.

Then again, maybe,
I'll just clean up her mess.

Who's been in the bathroom,
they'll just have to guess.

Who's used the shampoo
and the back scrubber, too?

They'd never believe
it's a bear from the zoo!

26

But now I know,
bears like being clean, too.

Both bears from the woods
and bears from the zoo.

My bear is all set now
for her long winter's sleep.

A long and CLEAN
winter's sleep in the deep.

THE END

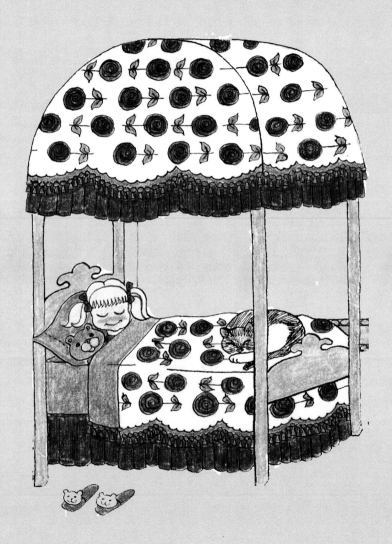

Enjoy another book of playful rhymes and whimsical illustrations

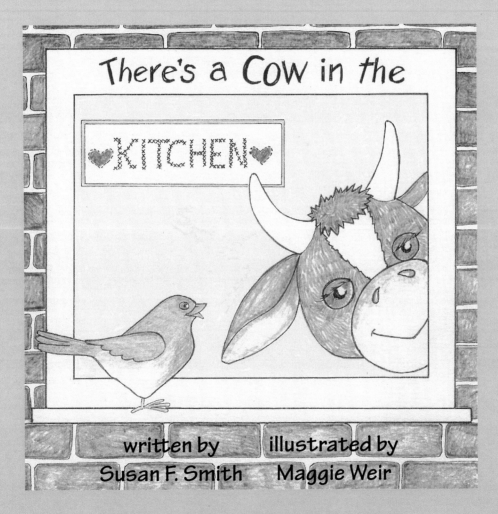

There's a COW in the

♥KITCHEN♥

written by   illustrated by
Susan F. Smith   Maggie Weir

ISBN: 978-1-936172-20-7

Meet the author and illustrator:

 Susan F. Smith is a former elementary school teacher and dedicated pre-school volunteer. She is also a community leader, activist, and loving grandmother. Sue's interest in children's literature goes back to the 1960s when she was teaching first grade and penned this poem along with several others. Now she volunteers in her grandchildren's school libraries and loves reading aloud to children.

 Maggie Weir graduated from the University of Iowa with a degree in art and elementary education. She is known for her whimsical animal murals in local buildings and for her "trompe l'oeil" creations on cutting boards and furniture. Maggie is curator of the Door County Historical Museum in Sturgeon Bay, WI, and a "Puppy Counselor" for Leader Dogs for the Blind. She and her husband, Jeff, are currently raising their 20th Leader Dog pup.